海豚双语童书经典回放
Classical Playback of Dolphin Bilingual Children's Books

The Fox Family

狐狸家族

海豚出版社
DOLPHIN BOOKS
CIPG 中国国际出版集团

海豚双语童书经典回放

图书在版编目（CIP）数据

狐狸家族：汉英对照 / 黄衣青著. -- 北京：海豚出版社, 2015.3
（海豚双语童书经典回放）
ISBN 978-7-5110-1001-8

Ⅰ. ①狐… Ⅱ. ①黄… Ⅲ. ①儿童文学—图画故事—中国—当代 Ⅳ. ①I287.8

中国版本图书馆CIP数据核字(2015)第035538号

书　　名：海豚双语童书经典回放·狐狸家族
作　　者：黄衣青

总发行人：俞晓群

责任编辑：李忠孝　陈三霞　李宏声
责任印制：王瑞松
出　　版：海豚出版社有限责任公司
网　　址：http://www.dolphin-books.com.cn
地　　址：北京市西城区百万庄大街24号
邮　　编：100037
电　　话：010-68997480（销售）　010-68998879（总编室）
传　　真：010-68998879
印　　刷：北京捷迅佳彩印刷有限公司
经　　销：新华书店及网络书店
开　　本：16开（710毫米×960毫米）
印　　张：1.375　　字　　数：5千
印　　数：5000
版　　次：2015年3月第1版　　2015年3月第1次印刷
标准书号：ISBN 978-7-5110-1001-8
定　　价：17.00元

In the spring, Mother Fox gave birth to five little cubs. She was very happy.

In a little while the cubs grew bigger. When Mother Fox didn't have enough milk for them, Father Fox would venture out to catch small animals to feed the little cubs.

春天，狐狸妈妈生了五只小狐狸，她非常高兴。

很快，几只小狐狸长得越来越大了。当狐狸妈妈没有足够的奶水喂他们时，狐狸爸爸会冒险去捕捉小动物来喂养他们。

Sometimes Father Fox would return with five frogs, and sometimes he would return with five field mice, one for each of the five cubs.

有时，狐狸爸爸带回五只青蛙，有时他会带回五只田鼠，五只小狐狸每只各一份。

One evening, Father Fox said to Mother Fox and their cubs: "Wait at home for me. I'll go and get you something to eat."

一天晚上，狐狸爸爸对狐狸妈妈和小狐狸们说："在家等着我，我要给你们带回一些食物。"

They waited for a whole night. Father Fox came back with a single pheasant.

"Say thank you to your daddy," said Mother Fox. "He must be very tired."

When Mother Fox and the cubs ate the tender and delicious pheasant, they felt very contented.

他们等了一整夜。狐狸爸爸带回来了一只野鸡。

"跟爸爸说谢谢，"狐狸妈妈对小狐狸们说，"他一定非常累！"

当狐狸妈妈和小狐狸们吃着鲜嫩美味的野鸡时，一家人感到非常满足。

Another day, Father and Mother Fox went to the forest in search of food.

All of a sudden, a hare ran past. Father Fox sprang on the hare and caught it.

有一天，狐狸爸爸和狐狸妈妈到森林里寻找食物。
突然，一只野兔跑了出来。狐狸爸爸扑向野兔，抓住了它。

The five little cubs were so hungry that they all threw themselves on the hare. In the twinkling of an eye they had eaten it up.

Then Father Fox went out again to search for food. He searched for a long time before he scented field mouse at a treehole.

饥饿的五只小狐狸全都扑到了野兔身上。一眨眼的工夫， 野兔就被吃光了。

然后，狐狸爸爸再一次出去寻找食物。他找了很长时间，直到他在一个树洞里嗅到了田鼠的味道。

After a little while, a field mouse stretched its head out of the hole, and Father Fox pounced on it and caught it.

"Let's tear it up into five pieces," Mother Fox said to Father Fox, "and bury them in different places. Then we'll see if our cubs can scent them or not."

过了一会儿，一只田鼠从树洞里探出头来，狐狸爸爸扑过去抓住了它。

"我们把它分成五份，"狐狸妈妈对狐狸爸爸说，"再把它们埋到不同的地方。然后，看看我们的孩子能不能闻到它们的味道。"

The five little fox-cubs sniffed at the ground for just a little while, before starting to scream: "I've scented it!" "I've scented it!"

"Look," Father Fox remarked happily, "our children can find food by themselves!"

五只小狐狸在地上嗅了一会儿，便开始尖叫："我嗅到它了！""我嗅到它了！"

"看！"狐狸爸爸开心地说，"我们的孩子能自己找到食物了！"

When winter arrived, some animals went south. Some orhers remained in their lairs and hibernated throughout the winter. Since the foxes had nothing to eat, they had to migrate.

On the day they were due to depart, they set out at day-break. With Father Fox leading, the whole family walked quietly along a short-cut, so as to avoid being seen by hunters.

冬天来了，一些动物去了南方；另一些动物待在自己的洞穴里冬眠过冬。因此，狐狸们没有足够多的吃的东西，他们必须迁移。

离开的那天，他们在破晓时分就出发了。为了不被猎人看到，由狐狸爸爸带领着，全家人沿着捷径悄悄地走着。

On their way, Father Fox caught the scent of a field mouse. He imitated the call of the mouse in order to entice it out of its hole. Sure enough, the mouse crawled out of the hole and was caught.

The five little foxes learned many tricks along the way. They were very happy.

在路上，狐狸爸爸嗅到了田鼠的味道。他模仿田鼠的声音诱骗田鼠们从洞里爬出来。果然，田鼠爬出了洞，被狐狸爸爸逮住了。

五只小狐狸一路上学习了很多招数，这让他们非常开心。

All of a sudden, Father Fox spotted a hunter. He asked Mother Fox and the cubs to hide behind a large rock. Then he went ahead to distract the hunter's attention.

A few months had elapsed. The five little fox cubs were now all fully-grown, and had learnt to fend for them selves.

突然，狐狸爸爸被猎人发现了。他把狐狸妈妈和小狐狸们藏到大石头后面，他自己冲了出去引开猎人的注意力。

几个月过去了，五只小狐狸都长大了，他们都学会了怎样谋生。